the 53rd

State

Occasional

no. 1

53SP 17
June 2013

ISBN no. 978-0-9857577-4-8
Library of Congress Control no. 2013939556

53rdstatepress.org

edited by
PAUL LAZAR

June 2013

53rd State Press
Brooklyn, New York

with responses from
JESS BARBAGALLO
TYMBERLY CANALE
STEVE CUIFFO
ERIC DYER
ERIK EHN
JIM FINDLAY
DAYNA HANSON
KEITH HENNESSY
MOLLY HICKOCK
KRISTEN KOSMAS
YOUNG JEAN LEE
TREY LYFORD
KIRK LYNN
ANNIE-B PARSON
KOURTNEY RUTHERFORD
TINA SATTER
SHEENA SEE
SCOTT SHEPHERD
PETE SIMPSON
GEOFF SOBELLE
SUZIE SOKOL
& KARINNE KEITHLEY SYERS

Each edition of the *Occasional* invites a guest editor to talk with artists, thinkers and members of our community about questions that we have and topics that move us.

In this inaugural issue, Paul Lazar asks:

What matters most?

How did I come up with this question? Good question. Really, it came to me in a picture rather than a thought; in my mind's eye, I imagined many of the theater makers that I most admire. I enjoyed this imagining. These faces are open, honest, spirited, tricky and deliciously perverse. These are the faces of people who are driven. And though I'm invigorated by such spirit and relentless drive it makes me want to ask: what is the single thing that is the most important thing for your work to do? More precisely, if you made a piece that failed in every way but one what would you need that one successful thing to be and do?

This leads me to wonder, are there things endemic to our community that create obstacles to getting at what matters most to you? What about the non-traditional theater, or the downtown community, or what you will, spawns a misgiving, evokes a frustration, creates an impediment to that thing you want your work to do? I'm not speaking so much of financial impediments, but of conceptual or methodological ones. There is much about the downtown theater that makes it possible to get at that thing. But all communities have a certain tendency toward mutual self-congratulation, and we are not immune. I know that I itch with ambivalence about aspects of our community, and that if I were asked to express my misgivings I would feel disturbed by that question, disturbed in a valid way. I would be at once hesitant to answer and desirous to put words to that which I feel distinctly but seldom acknowledge. Maybe this question might spawn a bit of constructive discord. Maybe not. Nonetheless I wonder: where do you part ways with your people?

This is a question in two moods. You can choose which mood to respond to. What matters most? Where do you part ways with your people? I'm asking because I really want to know.

JESS BARBAGALLO

I want my work to be something that cannot quite be placed. You walk into a room and a thing is happening that is a mystery. This does not mean it is not familiar. Maybe you have stepped into this space or scenario or sequence many times before. You know it's "theater," I guess—an event is happening or about to ensue. Sometimes, slyly, you arrive as it completes. You sit, you stand, you wait, twiddle, palpitate. And just as you've made some adjustment to new circumstance, expectation is dashed. Something goes awry. A thing spills forth in front of you that your mind cannot keep up with. Why has this mixture of substances and textures come together? It is hard to say whether the parts are even complementing one another, it's almost unpleasant. Chin stroke: A foot in Dada, perhaps... a sequence of actions and characters rolling out... every element just left of its proper place. And so you are in the midst of something very jankety and trying very hard to locate and assign just who is the alien—me? them? the event?—so strange is this just-left feeling. Strange... the other foot could be in the now-not-weirdo Brecht. But when you lean forward to inquire, this historical footing is no help and you actually fall on the stage. A moving image:

you/me dumbly falling/
you/me gently hitting/
your/my head

* * *

Active attempts to "re-invent theater" negatively
trouble the theater—I think of this as intellectual
frustration devoid of spiritual investigation. These
days, I like my manifestoes and polemics to the
side of my theater... I have found myself shivering
at buzzwords like "conceptual framework" and
"rigor," categories like "queer art" and "dance theater." It is not that I completely disrespect these
classes or descriptors. I only wish they could each
be explicitly modified by the phrase "bound to
change" until they are implicitly received as such.

* * *

Innovation is one of the least interesting aesthetic
manifestations of the science fiction principle.
Take, for example, the once-revolutionary notion
to steal from the cinema. The persistence of this
appropriation has actually led to a foreclosure on
theatrical creativity and become an unavoidable
trope and immediate association of the avant-
garde. Montage is a feeling-substitute. Soundtrack

is a cueing device. Constructed pause is the ugly simulacrum of quiet. The fissures now are only the clunkiness of operations, so the dreams have become skewed:

How well can stagecraft deceive actuality?

How many beats do I count between the lines before I've fully anesthetized the wild heart?

* * *

Some dictums:

1. The trek towards the framed live should never be a moot journey, or you're doing a shitty job as a host;

2. The X-factor of performance should never be the victory of digital technology on a given evening (i.e. a shortcut);

3. The assumption that we are so versed in jump cut that the interstitial is dismissible is a dismissible assumption;

4. The tenderness of a fully evoked tedium, or the passage of silence: these are special and theatrical things.

TYMBERLY CANALE

Writing things down seems so permanent, so defined. I am not naturally drawn to things that can be defined, nor the process of it. I think this is because my childhood was a haze due to domestic violence in my household. I think I needed to create a haze, a forgetfulness, a non-attachment to get through it. I think this has affected what I like, what I make and my presence in the work I do.

I suppose it is obvious to say that the work I make and the work I like reflects my past history. I like performance pieces that approach a subject not quite head-on, that has multiple meanings that is expressed through rhythm (either of speech or through physicality). I like careful, clean, wild beauty on stage that shows the seams, or the fault lines of the work. I suppose that in pieces here and there sprinkled through over 20 years of performing, there are parts of my history within. Some other things about me that inform my presence on stage or in our "community":

I don't like crowds.

I don't have a good memory (not about retaining movement or words from a play but about real life facts and things that occurred).

I am an only child, so I like it when people look at me.

I am a little sickly and I tend to dwell in the drama of my illnesses/physical problems.

I am empathetic, perhaps dangerously so. I have to keep a check on this because I can become too involved. And not spend my time well.

I am loyal like there's no tomorrow.

Since I am getting so down, dirty and personal here, one might assume that getting closer to others is the motivation for why I perform. But still, at the essence, in a room full of people in the lobby of a theater, I don't feel like I belong or am close to anyone. I'm not even really sure how to try at that in our community. I stumble and mutter and say goofy things. I don't go to nearly enough shows, as I've got a wonderful kid and husband at home. So where is the closeness through my work? It's my fellow performers that I come to rely on in very personal, meaningful ways. There is deep and important love that is different than my family but deep like that. I find it harder to be my true self off of the stage, but I think that's common in performers. I like the "plan" of a performance and confronting the changing variables within. But in the lobby at other people's shows, I feel judgment and competitiveness. I don't want to, but I do. I feel out of place. I feel like I don't belong. I know this is likely due to my own history but I wonder how many other people in the experimental theater and dance community feel the same way.

STEVE CUIFFO

There seems to be an expectation for work to have "value" other than itself, whether it be literary, academic, or have some socially redeeming quality to it. Perhaps this has to do with writing grants and having to articulate what something is before it exists in order to get support to begin the real creative process. Using sleight of hand, magic, imitation, re-enactment and other techniques, I try to create work that expresses my point of view through live performance. If I can truthfully convey my unique insight into some theme or idea, I have succeeded. Art and performance can have many effects on an audience, i.e. sparking debate, causing social change, raising political awareness, etc., but those things are not essential. If all of that failed, the art would still exist in and of itself and that is what is most important. It need not have any other purpose than that. It's transcendence through performance, and it's worthwhile because IT IS.

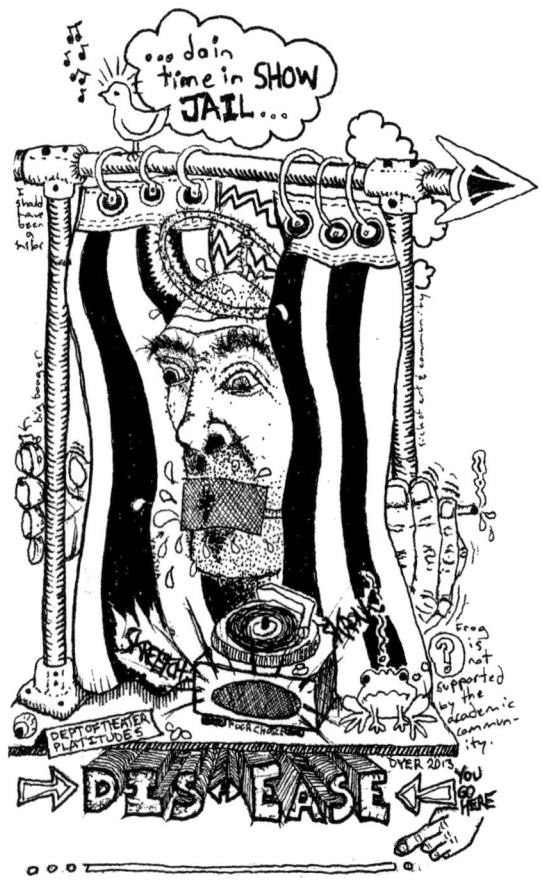

ERIK EHN

Something about donation. About providing the grounds in safety or the imperative in threat and shock to leave where one is and go where it is. This takes the diatribe of silence, the rage of patience (anger being the most patient driver; anger-teacher), the thievery in perseverance which respects no boundary. What's most important is that we give ourselves away, in the senses of: ruin and spill, self-betrayal, at no cost (except what people elect to part with; an ethical expense; the performance making a public space in which hearts can effect their most meaningful change, turning out from private property to shared property). Theater itself needs a change of heart, which means – it needs to find a way to operate in public space, and we've made our spaces private. The person of theater can't experience what's most important in theater – can't give itself away, can't reveal its own lies. Unless we find way to operate in public and in freedom, we'll remain personalities; personality is procrastination; solitaire. Public space is shrinking everywhere and freedom is cancered, fibrously and affectively. What I need, materially, to live, I'll need to earn and pay for. What I need spiritually, will be given to me and not because I've earned it. What I need to give (to move beyond procrastination, from I to the time-right-now) has to be given with no end in sight other than the end of sight. Something about the deep dark.

JIM FINDLAY

I would need it to fail in that one last way too.

The work is at the end about the distance between what it reaches for and the end of its reach. Getting close is important. The full effort to arrive is the necessary impulse that drives us on. But to arrive? That is the most deadly. To have zero space between you/me/I/us and what you/me/I/us might be reaching for. THAT feels like an end. The end. And that disturbs the impulse to go on making more than any other threat. To feel that I "know" something feels like murder. While I'm reaching, it feels like love, because it's all desire and it's hot and sticky and it's pulling me through a tiny hole to get there. And the pressure rises and rises like putting your finger over the end of the hose. But when I get there, the only thing left is to wrap my fingers around your throat and squeeze, because that's what love does, and then I can just fucking squeeze the life out of your neck like a tube of toothpaste. And killing you is a mistake, but it is the absolute ugly truth of who I really am. I hope you would do the same.

Murder is the only real end. After that it's finally freedom. From being human. From trying. A vast and perfect future space of no god no life no society no tribe. A real solo.

DAYNA HANSON

As human beings creating theater and dance—
live art—our work is inherently reflexive. Humans
are our medium of expression as well as our
subject matter. Reflecting human behavior and
experience effectively is difficult, for people are
infinitely untidy, contradictory and mysterious.
As art-makers, we are those things as well. It's as
hard to transpose our perspective on the human
experience to the stage as it is to look in the
mirror and know how others see us.

What matters most is continually striving to get
that humanity part right—even more, perhaps,
than actually getting it right—striving, without
surefire methods, to be faithful to ourselves. No
formula exists to aid us. Craft, talent and skill
are helpful but really these resources, along with
virtuosity, are present to serve intuition. Crucial
components in a sound and flexible apparatus for
the free flow of intuition.

Not that we shouldn't be smart, shouldn't reason
or formulate. But our ability to understand without
thinking has as much value in our quest for the
truth of human experience as it does in all other

realms of our lives. That which emerges from the lower levels of our consciousness tends to have more deep tone, tends to guide us well, especially when we're smart enough to discern it.

In our absorption we may overlook the fact that we are at the heart of what we trade in. Engaged in the inconstant marketplace of contemporary performance we can forget how high the stakes really are. In art as in the human experience, being real is the only viable option. So we bring humble awareness of the vanity, impossibility and necessity of our work and we show ourselves.

KEITH HENNESSY

What matters most? No yelling on the job, by anyone, at anyone (unless the job is yelling while performing, playing, improvising, acting). Yelling belongs to some kind of diva drama artist hero shit that I am against. Every project has to be good for everyone in the project. My goal is to inspire and instigate the conditions in which everyone can move, be moved, feel moved, take a step in a good direction, look for opportunities for each other, learn, unlearn, shift, break, remake, come out, heal and/or change.

I like to do the obvious: to cry, to scream fuck you, to re-present torture, to take off my clothes (or yours), to threaten violence, to flirt with danger. I'm kneejerk, heart on sleeve, first degree. I don't work from the inside out. I work from the outside in. This is merely a tactic for the tougher task of rejecting or disrupting the binary of inside/outside. I re/search until I find something on the outside that resonates with what I haven't paid attention to on the inside. I focus there but notice what's happening here. Once a project is moving I experience the world differently, with more curiosity and engagement, with more wonder and love, with more attention to solidarity and mutual aid. It seems like art is useless and political art is always already a failure, until I listen more closely and truly see what's happening around me. I do this listening and noticing best when making or experiencing live performance.

MOLLY HICKOK

Downtown theater spent decades taking everything apart—narrative, character, the 4th wall, the audience, structure, language, etc. It was a wonderful explosion of creativity. What with immersive theater and the white box and whatever, I guess the explosion is still happening? But sometimes the rhetoric sounds a bit desperate. We talk about our work as "cutting edge" or "new," but it doesn't feel new. It's tiresome to always have to be touting something as new when it's not. Why can't we be allowed to admit that our form has matured and now has all of its own comforts and crochets and conventions. And our conventions are rich! They are now being taught to and digested by a whole new generation of artists. There is a lot of life left in those conventions. It's just not the same kind of life as when they first came on the scene.

When you fall out of love with your partner, I guess it's natural to castigate as much as possible, so you can pretend it's all their fault. I find myself castigating all the time: downtown theater bores me to death—another deconstruction, another self-referential circle, another clever, "imaginative" staging idea! It's such a middle-aged thing to do, but downtown theater is no longer young and neither am I. It's hard not to corrode in middle-age. I don't want to be corroded, but I have corroded.

I fell out of love with the downtown scene because I increasingly found myself to be concerned with grants and gigs and reviews. My colleagues liked things that I found tedious. When I finally got to fly to France or Germany and perform in those wonderful theaters, I was very happy. But then all of a sudden I found it completely pointless. The amount of carbon being produced to fly art around the world began to bother me. I stopped enjoying the international art circuit. It seemed glamorous from the outside but from the inside it became just another airport. I began to get tired of my own professional ambitions and I no longer had any artistic ones. I couldn't invent anything—I literally couldn't move.

I think a lot about Ron Vawter. I look at someone like Sibyl Kempson and am in awe of the dynamo inside her. I think about when she did *Crime or Emergency* at Dixon Place. The piece wasn't for anyone except those of us gathered in the room. I loved rainpan 43's *Elephant Room* for the same reason. The play was not "meaningful" in the usual sense but the magic was magical in a way that was kind of better than being meaningful in the way we usually practice it. I really wish I had some of Sibyl's madness and energy left in me. Or that I wanted to practice a magic trick 250 times and make it perfect. I am at a late middle-aged loss and that's the truth.

When this horrible malaise descended I couldn't find anything in the downtown art world that could see me through. This makes me very sad, because it seems that creativity is one of the things that makes life meaningful and downtown is filled with creativity. It is a mystery to me why my own world couldn't see me through, because it has certainly sustained others.

I think this is what matters most to me, what I would want to succeed if everything else I was trying to do failed (and there is a lot of other stuff I am trying to do). But if everything else failed, I think I would want this to be the one thing that worked. And I do think it's a place where I part company with many of my friends, peers, colleagues, and heroes. I'm neither proud nor ashamed of it. Or maybe I'm a little ashamed. Or embarrassed. But I think this is in fact what I'm inclined and given to do. Maybe because it's the thing I most need done. I don't know.

uplift

verb |ˌəpˈlift| [trans.]

1 [usu. as adj.] (uplifted) lift (something) up; raise : her uplifted face.

• (be uplifted) (of an island, mountain, etc.) be created by an upward movement of the earth's surface.

2 elevate or stimulate (someone) morally or spiritually : [as adj.] (uplifting) an uplifting tune.

noun |ˈəpˌlift| |ˈəpˈlɪft| |ˈʌplɪft|

1 an act of raising something.

• *Geology* the upward movement of part of the earth's surface.

• [often as adj.] support, esp. for a woman's bust, from a garment : an uplift bra.

2 a morally or spiritually elevating influence : their love will prove an enormous uplift.

derivatives

uplifter |ˌəpˈliftər| |ˈəpˈlɪftər| |-ˈlɪftə| noun

YOUNG JEAN LEE

What matters most in my work is trying to figure out ways to get people to consider and engage with things they want to dismiss. I part ways with my people when they resist and condemn any deviation from the current conventions of experimental theater.

TREY LYFORD

At the risk of sounding completely sentimental, people are what matters most. The people in the room. The energy and enjoyment coming from the people in the rehearsal, in the tech rehearsal and in the audience. They all shape and form what I do. But also the people we are trying to portray onstage. No matter how idiotic and obtuse they become, they need to have something in them that allows us in. They need to be people too. Vulnerable people that help us see, "Oh right, I'm not the only asshole idiot on the bus. There's these guys too!"

That's truly what inspires me to continue to do what I do. For me it's the reason most of our work exists without a fourth wall. We are always playing with and to the people who are there that night. This isn't just a rule of the form. It's an ethical commitment. I see you! We are in this thing together. I love playing in a tiny, packed house filled with pillars and dust and old chairs and just celebrating what it feels like to not be on Facebook.

In reality, I am so busy being a dad and getting to rehearsal on time that when I am there I'm just trying to make things that make me laugh and feel something. So even though I create for the people in the room, there is only so much of that you can do. I learned fairly early on that trying to make work with other people's taste in mind can be a real challenge. I realize it's common knowledge, but you can only make work for yourself. And if you are lucky, someone else will see the world the way you do.

What I love most about the theater community that we are a part of is I think audiences and other artists are open to what is possible. How else can you say something? What can you do to express a moment in a different way? That said, the tenacious drive of downtown artists to find new forms of expression can be dangerous. Sometimes the Simple vanishes. I'm all for complication and layering, but you have to break that rhythm. I like to search for those moments inside the chaos when you can say something simply. There are times when an uncluttered moment can be more avant garde than the avant garde. The other thing I find less interesting than others is a contemporary obsession with technology. In the end, if it can be analog it just feels more alive to me. If it's in the space for real, it has more imaginative possibility. I'd rather see you try to make an ocean landscape out of saran wrap and kool aid than projecting it on a scrim or sheet. I think my preference here is just another example of how I love being in the room together. There is enough virtual representation in our lives. I prefer the real thing.

KIRK LYNN

Self-Instructions to Help Me Find What Matters Most

The Simple Room

Empty out one room of your house, if you have more than one room. If not, use a large cardboard box. This will be your simple room. Spend as much time as you can in the simple room. You can do anything you normally do, but if you do it in the simple room you can only bring in one item at a time. You can bring a chair into the simple room for sitting. You can read a book in the simple room, but then no chair, no lamp. You can only read during the day. You can eat in the simple room, but no plates, no silverware. Spend as much time as you can in the simple room. You can write in the simple room. Bring in a pencil, write on the walls. You can bring a camera into the simple room to take pictures of the walls to get your writing out. You can perform a play in the simple room. If your play has no set and no costumes and no props you can invite in an audience, one person at a time.

Three Victories are Possible with Two People

You and someone else begin in separate rooms with felt-tipped pens. Make a single dot anywhere on your bodies. Come together. Look for the dot on one another, tenderly. Finding the other dot is one victory. To have your own dot found is a second victory. And a third victory is possible.

The Strange Hour

Pick an hour of the week, every week, and the only rule for that hour is you cannot be with anyone you know, you cannot be in a place you know, and you cannot be doing anything you know how to do. Force yourself into other parts of the city, into other people's lives, into new competencies and failures.

Ask for Something Easy

At the beginning of your lunch hour, leave a small little note somewhere it will be found. Taped to the back of a stall in a bathroom. Ask for something easy. For instance, ask someone to walk down to the atrium, to the center of the room, and drop a penny on the floor and then pick it up. Meanwhile, go eat lunch somewhere you can watch and see if you get your show. Even if no one performs for you, you still get to wait to see if it happens.

Magic and Mistakes

Pour yourself a glass of water. Pour that glass of water into another glass. Pour it back and forth. Do this as often as you can. How many days does the water last? Do it with a group of people. Listen to the sound. Does most of the water disappear by spilling or by evaporation? What about your life? Does most of it go away because of mistakes you've made? Or by the magic of entertainment?

ANNIE-B PARSON

"We in the theater are thieves, we steal from dance."

—*Ron Vawter, on accepting a Bessie Award*

Stillness and lack of emotion are everywhere right now in downtown theater — The New Factualism, I call it. But in the 1960's (50 years ago!), when the Judson Church choreographers reinvented beauty in task-based-pedestrianism, the neutrality of body and soul was ubiquitous, expressive, new and beautiful. This factuality was expressive in theater when Rich Maxwell staged his play *HOUSE* in 1998, but it is not the answer to staging and speaking all things. So where I lovingly part ways with my downtown theater friends is in their trending toward an undying patriotism toward emotional neutrality and non-motion. I see too much derivative work by young directors, performances that look like two dimensional stick figures doing cheerleading moves, if they move at all.

But, I saw a duet the other night, a dance of two young men. It was non-narrative, it was emotional and maybe the most romantic work I have seen downtown in years. The body was presented as multi-dimensional, and it felt risky and real. Like *HOUSE* felt in 1998.

What matters? Shape, space, motion, emotion, time, and rhythm. Movement matters. Manipulating movement and text matters. What matters is matter, materiality.

KOURTNEY RUTHERFORD

I really think great theater takes us to a place where nothing matters but what is happening in that room. This is a tough thing to tackle, but it's what I really try to transmit as a performer, and it is also the stuff that I like to watch. Shows I like take me to a place where I am different from who I am when I am walking around in the world.

What I appreciate about the experimental or downtown approach is that it is much more open to the notion that theater can be an art form that is super primary, yet layered and compound. There is room for a lot of interests. Lots of attention is paid to formal elements like design, sound, the look of a thing. It also freely incorporates other forms that are whole unto themselves like dance and music. I realize that straight plays do all that stuff too. However, working our way permits trying a lot of things we wouldn't be able to try otherwise. I've seen dancers become actors, playwrights learn Norwegian—all this in service of engaging with solving some problem. The play needed them to do this, and it was done. I really like the spirit of that—it makes it seem like anything is possible.

I feel a lot of people get dispirited and crap out on their work because there is always a trade-off between freedom and security. You are given this great gift of doing whatever you want in service of an idea, but there is a serious downside. Barring the financial constraints, there may not be an audience for what you are doing—they might be hung up on a notion of what a piece of theater should do or be for them. Or you can't get someone like a presenter to even look at what you do. Maybe you experience whatever success is in this mode and you have to artificially create tension in order to feel like you're working.

I saw the coolest play recently, during which I had some insight into all this. My friend the playwright Kenny Finkle has been working on a side project "U R Star" when he has been in between regular theater gigs. This show is a musical that is a portfolio of childlike drawings and played along with a soundtrack. Kenny did all the art and the music. He sits right there as you experience the show.

Kenny's a friend, so we chatted and caught up, but I was honestly preoccupied by my busy, boring, real life. As I started listening to and looking at the show, however, something changed. It was only me there, and only him—no audience, no economy, no frustrations. As I watched and listened with Kenny, I remembered that someone puts hours into making everything we see. It's understandable for them to lose heart if people aren't looking: what matters most is what happens in the moments when both of us are.

TINA SATTER

I want the art I see and make to be like slyly totally fucked, quiet, loud, weird and extrasensory missives from another dimension that is actually the real one inside us and around us (& we just might not have known yet). That is what I want first and foremost in what I see and make in art contexts. So it is about Possibility and beyond what is the usually visible.

Potential Constructive Discord. Since Paul asked! I have a hard time feeling a spiritual pull towards the specific insistence of late across many aspects of theater-making that the core value of theater work is a delineated social mission.

Of course in one layer that is what art always is. The personal/art is political. I am a Feminist who believes that. But the codifications around social message value in theatrical contexts are for the most part being defined in simplified and potentially deadening terms. Deadening to the art, and for the way art can and should function (offering reconfigured conceptions that come out of it, not always just reflecting back). Maybe my distrust of this thread is a matter of taste. And that's another grapple. I have a million questions to ask to my brain and to the world.

I do believe in humans, work, possibility, fairness, and in making huge mistakes and incredible leaps of stupid, sublime faith to create something real that happens. Where at least one molecule/moment/section (maybe more—the whole thing) pops out, curves out and around and above or from inside it (or you) to feel like nothing else you know and coming from deep inside everything you know. And this comes from the rigor of human beings being there within an aesthetic, physical, textual, and feeling-based constraint that is the laboratory for arranging these molecules and creating these moments. So that is about a sense that something can happen. Something can be made. Something can be changed.

SHEENA SEE

Well, the first rule of theater is… well, you know the rest.

It is a kind of private thing. Hard to talk about. It is like explaining comedy. When you try, it certainly isn't about comedy or what comedy is. You can't explain it, you just have to do it. Some people are just driven to do it. To make things. What matters most on a very literal level is to be heard and to be seen. Usually what is good is made by people who don't try to explain it, they just put it out there let people see it. Is that about some kind of ego trip? I hope not. That is what gets in the way. You have to do it with other people (usually) and then egos—usually theirs—just get in the way.

What makes it work, what makes it matter, is hard to put into words. Theater people should just make theater and not try talk about it too much. Theater and art are mysteries and should remain that way for their magic to work. And all these awards given to theater people, what is that all about? Art shouldn't be a competition. And how can it be judged? And who cares?

The fact that theater is an ephemeral art form is important to its survival. You have to BE THERE and see it with a bunch of other people. It only remains in memory. That is what makes it so powerful.

The end.

SCOTT SHEPHERD

It's a vexing question, "what matters?" because it points straight to the worry that some of us in our weaker moments (and I won't name names) are vulnerable to: does this even matter?

I mean presumably if you've ended up in the less lucrative arts you must have once been in the presence of some work of art that made you think, this matters. Some confusion or distraction dropped away and allowed you a momentary deeper insight into the human predicament or some such thing, and that's why you wound up here instead of doing something utilitarian with your life.

Anyway this is the best answer I've got: you believe that a transcendent experience is possible and you're trying to set up conditions under which that can occur. It's never clear exactly how to do that so you spend your career repeatedly trying to figure it out. And what matters is that it continues to matter to you.

PETE SIMPSON

What matters most might be to elucidate/confront/subvert the viewer's ANCIENTLY reflexive presumption that the communication potential of theater is somehow formally limited, predictable or safe. Nothing radical there, but I think the constant care and maintenance required to dismantle that presumption is a more natural component of our downtown work than other theater aesthetic systems..

I'd like people to experience giddiness. They can hate it, but if they've felt giddy for even a moment, I've succeeded. I just looked up the word "giddy" and that affirms it for me: folk should feel—existentially— "1. lightheaded, vertiginous. 2. unstable, volatile, fickle, inconstant, vacillating" at least once, sustained for at least 5 consecutive seconds. (10 seconds?)

I've only produced self-written material once (which was filtered through a collaboration). We won a couple of awards and had fun, and it bolstered me to go solo; to write precisely wtf was in my mind and soul, regardless of how f'd up it might be. Writing it was as far as I got.

Never saw the light of day. The reason? A prosaic tale of cowardice and doubt (which is endemic to me, not—at least generally—to our community). I think the nature of my and some downtown artists' fear is that of peer opinion which, further decoded, is simply the fear of being derivative, confusing, boring, pulseless. And while those things certainly haunt artists of other idioms, I always assume someone writing, say, proper plays for Broadway somehow has less pressure to be bracingly original than to simply be an adroit manipulator of playwriting clichés, creating characters who voice their social criticisms or relationship insights with strategically ironic, sexy pith. So maybe there's some unique downtown pressure on artists to arrive in non-derivative and brilliant form right out the gates (ironic, considering how derivative and conveniently precursor-amnesiac our work can sometimes be). While I think we are each other's best audiences and express a great deal of enthusiasm for developing work, our community also has to own its sometimes presumptuous, jaded, cynical—even envious—mindset that can make first creative outings a hell for new artists, and for established artists, can make self-reinvention a little harder by enforcing a kind of tyrannical expectation for familiar forms.

Lastly, there's a downtown model that's mostly extinct but worth mentioning that I part ways with it: that of the cult of personality. This is a purely sentimental complaint on my part, but an icy, muscularly intellectual, over-codified, members-only, reference-dropping, loveless approach to work bothers me; the idea that edgy, confrontational, interestingly oblique work simply can't be generated without an edgy, confrontational process, and that participants must be ambitiously bent on how interestingly oblique they can—or should—be as people, seems like a waste of time. In the rare times I encounter it in myself or others, I feel like we should remind ourselves that while all the work we do can be amazing and will certainly make some book references and some important archives, it can't be so important as to justify such an awkwardly selective packaging of our humanity.

The single most important thing is to leave the room. But without actually leaving the room. It's a kind of magic trick. There you were—you were in the room, and then suddenly—you went somewhere else—and then suddenly you came back. And now everything feels a bit different. That's the single most important thing: this experience of having left the room without getting out of your chair.

There's not just one way to do it, or to get there —and, in fact, there are so many ways to do this thing, that it won't quite do to use the same road twice. Because then we may start to smell a pattern. And patterns, though useful, can lead to formula, and formulas are for physicians, and physicians are for holding the hull together for smooth sailing—helpful for regattas, but this is something different. I am looking for an interruption, a digression, a subversion, a mistake… Not a pattern, but a break in the pattern… a way to see the pattern from the flip side.

The painter, Charles Wilson Peale, put it like this: "…to be led away from familiar objects toward the unfamiliar—guided along, as it were, a chain of flowers into the mysteries of life."

Once I saw something like this. It was called "Ghost Clock" by a guy called Wendell Castle. If you see it in a gallery, your experience might be something like mine. I am wandering around an exhibit, and in the middle of the museum is a big mahogany grandfather clock, mostly covered by a sheet, tied tight in the middle by a cotton cord. Even though it's all covered up, I know just what it is—there's no denying it. I can see the lines of its form pressing through the cotton sheet… Standing there, hidden and imposing, a clock becomes a monument. And then I look at the little description that tells you, "oil and gouache, egg tempura, mixed media…" that kind of thing… and on the requisite list of ingredients is just ONE ingredient: bleached Honduras mahogany. And I look again at the cotton sheet covering the clock and realize that I see—though it's very subtle— wood grain. And then I realize: there is no clock. There is no sheet. There is no cord tying the sheet in the middle. I'm looking at a single piece of carved wood. Mahogany tamed and transformed completely into the form of a clock hidden beneath a cotton sheet... And then I'm just thrilled to pieces. Because I realize that what I thought I was seeing was not at all what I was seeing. And the revelation and its repercussions—THAT'S the artwork. He created an object that takes you on a simple and perfect journey of assumption, subversion and revelation. Like a joke. A transcendent joke. Just when you think you know what you're looking at, it reveals itself to be something else. Something perhaps more basic, more true. I find that quite graceful.

SUZIE SOKOL

What matters most or what keeps me going:

–Being in a company where I thankfully keep finding roles to play.

–Going outside the company for adventure— working with Tina Satter and Half Straddle these past two years was a perfect compliment to working with ERS.

–The faith that breakthroughs will happen. By now, I am used to the ratio of tough rehearsal to breakthroughs. Four hours of tough rehearsing can lead to a five minute break through.

What matters most or what is most important to me as a performer:

–Standing out and fitting in.

–Finding a hook, a way into a new part, something to revere, something new to study.

–Going in and out of having a mask onstage— hide and reveal, hide and reveal.

People and process matter the most. The work of art itself is really just evidence of the events that transpired in the physical and psychic spaces in which it was made. It is a trace. Sometimes the trace is a distinct entity, and sometimes it is just a shorthand record of the actions and intentions that aided my/our escape from the narrow band of experience we recognize in daily life. When a trace—a piece—is compelling and has a physical presence of its own, it is like a miracle! I wonder how it happened, even though I am totally aware of the steps and intentions and invention strategies that made the structure. This miracle is nothing more or less than the way we processed and originated the elements that became the piece. The way I/we looked into things became the piece. If the piece is able to hold itself together and continue to resonate with the way it came to be, then it is like a Portuguese man-o-war. It has become a living being comprised of other living beings. In the case of a piece for performance, these living beings are not only the people in it, but the words and the actions that arise in sequences and arrangements every time the piece occurs.

But this thing that matters so much doesn't stop with the artist(s) enacting these things. This thing actually needs to encounter an audience, to be tested in transit. Are the people and processes of a piece both weak and strong enough to risk failure or success in the delivery? Sure, the moment of transference from maker to witness is the killing and birthing moment! I/we can kill the thing before it is truly born if we have not discovered ourselves in the piece once it has been made. I/we as performers have to crack the code of performing it. We might have made it, but we might not know how to perform it in a way that lives. That is failure in performance, but not necessarily in creation. That is why I have to put people and process ahead of any kind of qualitative assessment of a piece, because I think that sometimes really great art doesn't always make its way neatly into a great piece—we have to go through more than one sometimes to find the form. It might be possible to make something that passes audience, peer, and critic tests without having a life as itself. But for me this would be a different thing than making art.

The person I part ways with most frequently is myself. I am working on that here in LA with people in a room. I embrace and reject myself completely while creating and destroying everything I think I am as a performer, creator, person. After doing this, I feel ready to begin or end something, and I usually find that both things are happening almost all of the time.

KARINNE KEITHLEY SYERS

Once I thought difficulty was necessary, a kind of contract to continually restart in the present moment the activity of being an audience. But now I realize that I use difficulty or really in my case something more like a thickety density, to guard my freedom to follow whim, to go floating, to experience delight, none of which are necessarily difficult things. In my experience the circuit of that whim is delicate and arises on the edges of the field of thought, so naturally habit, which we could oppose to difficulty insofar as it relaxes an anxiety about intelligibility or its absence, has a trouncing effect on the whole effort to get near it, a nearing whose emblematic figure could be a boy Nabokov chasing cabbage moths down spectral sentences.

I have in recent years been on a series of wanders, a gentle exile from my professional life: living away from my people, writing a dissertation in a field I don't expect to continue in, and most importantly working with kids who pretty much could give a shit about downtown New York, but who are still open to the weird surprise of the studio. One thing that's happened during this time is that my work (at least in my own estimation of it) has become less and less difficult. Is this because I have learned to love television? Maybe a little. But I think the freedom that was being protected all those years has just gone on floating, and away from the world of the downtown syntax, is just as happily thriving in other circuits.

I guess I'm saying that goodness is what that scene in *American Beauty* proposed: a plastic bag looping and whipping around gently in invisible tracks of air. I think the experience of that transit, that loop-de-loop, is what matters most. And while the room of performance is my very favorite place to experience that float, I think we need to consider that our great good fortune to become skilled at persisting until we find that free float was not something we built, is not a special genius, and is not something we are in rightful possession of, against our culture's zombie addictions of mind or the violence of circumstance that exists outside our happy trade. The freedom of experience that we channel into compositions has other possible venues, and I believe we need to participate in building more spaces for more people to experience more freedom. When I was in college, planning my entry into adult life, the thought of opening a small town dance studio represented not only a professional failure but a non-entry into the profession. It's not that I wish I had just gone and done that, but I wish when we say that our dancers need to get paid, which is not only a reference to the cost of living but also a measure of value in and to the world, it's because they are doing work that multiplies and proliferates the goodness in the world we live in and live off of. I imagine this can radiate out from the nurturing, initiating community we call downtown. But if we keep ourselves strictly within that community, then it seems to me that the obligation to value, in respect and in dollars, is a private and not a public matter. Our poverty, we should remember, is voluntary. Our genius, we should remember, is common.

Jess Barbagallo is a writer and performer of ambivalent pronoun and strong theatrical conviction, an event maker.

Tymberly Canale has performed and collaborated with Big Dance Theater since 1995.

Steve Cuiffo is an actor and magician who makes solo, as well as, collaborative works with other artists and theater companies. His work incorporates aspects of sleight of hand, misdirection, imitation and re-enactment.

Eric Dyer is a maker and co-founder of Radiohole, Inc.

Erik Ehn is Artistic Associate with the Theatre of Yugen, a graduate of New Dramatists, and current Director of Writing for Performance, Brown University.

Jim Findlay makes all kinds of performances and lives in Brooklyn with his two kids and awesome girlfriend.

Dayna Hanson is a choreographer, director and multi-disciplinary artist based in Seattle.

Inspired by improvisation, anarchism, San Francisco, dance, and witchcraft, **Keith Hennessy** works in and around dance and performance.

Molly Hickok is a long-time member of Big Dance Theater.

Kristen Kosmas is an American playwright, performer, and Assistant Professor of Theatre at Whitman College.

Paul Lazar is an actor and co-director of Big Dance Theater; most recently he directed *Man in a Case* (Chekhov), *Ich, KurbisGeist* (Sibyl Kempson), *Elehpant Room*, and *We're Gonna Die* (Young Jean Lee).

Young Jean Lee is the artistic director of Young Jean Lee's Theater Company, which has presented her work in over twenty-five cities around the world.

Kirk Lynn lives in Austin, TX with his wife, the poet, Carrie Fountain, and their daughter, Olive Lynn Fountain—and any day now they'll be joined by a boy-baby whose name is still up in the air.

Trey Lyford is a father and the Co-Artistic Director of rainpan 43 performance group. He has created and performed in all of their works to date: *all wear bowlers*, *Amnesia Curiosa*, *machines machines machines machines machines machines machines* and *Elephant Room*.

Annie-B Parson is co-artistic director of Big Dance Theater. She also makes dance for plays, opera, and pop music.

Kourtney Rutherford lives in New York City, teaches high school, and performs with groups such as Big Dance Theater, Half Straddle, and Witness Relocation.

Tina Satter makes plays, performances, videos, music, and more with her company Half Straddle.

Scott Shepherd is a performer with The Wooster Group and Elevator Repair Service.

Pete Simpson is a veteran performer for many of NY's most acclaimed experimental theater directors, choreographers and companies, and continues his decade-and-a-half involvement as performer, trainer, and collaborator with the Blue Man Group.

Geoff Sobelle is the co-artistic director of rainpan 43, a renegade absurdist outfit devoted to creating original actor-driven performance works; using illusion, film and out-dated mechanics, R43 creates surreal, poetic pieces that look for humanity where you least expect it and find grace where no one is looking.

Susie Sokol is a second-grade teacher at St. Ann's School in Brooklyn and has been performing with Elevator Repair Service since 1992.

Stacy Dawson Stearns is an artist who uses her body to explore consciousness and to challenge physical restrictions inherent in capitalized, mediated society.

Karinne Keithley Syers has been making dance, sound, animation, books, and things that resemble plays from a distance, in and out of New York City, for nearly 20 years.

Book layout and design: Karinne Keithley Syers. Cover image: "Planetary Movement" by Unknown Astronomer (Public domain), via Wikimedia Commons. Printed on recycled paper.

53rd State Press publishes new writing for performance. It was founded in 2007 and is co-edited by Karinne Keithley Syers and Antje Oegel. For more information or to subscribe, visit 53rdstatepress.org. 53rd State Press books are distributed to the trade by TCG/Consortium.